Sarah the Sunday Fairy

by Daisy Meadows

illustrated by Georgie Ripper

ORCHARD

The Fairyland Palace
Time Tower
Windy Lake
The Tall Toy Store
Morristown Aquarium
Fountain
Dancing Days
Town

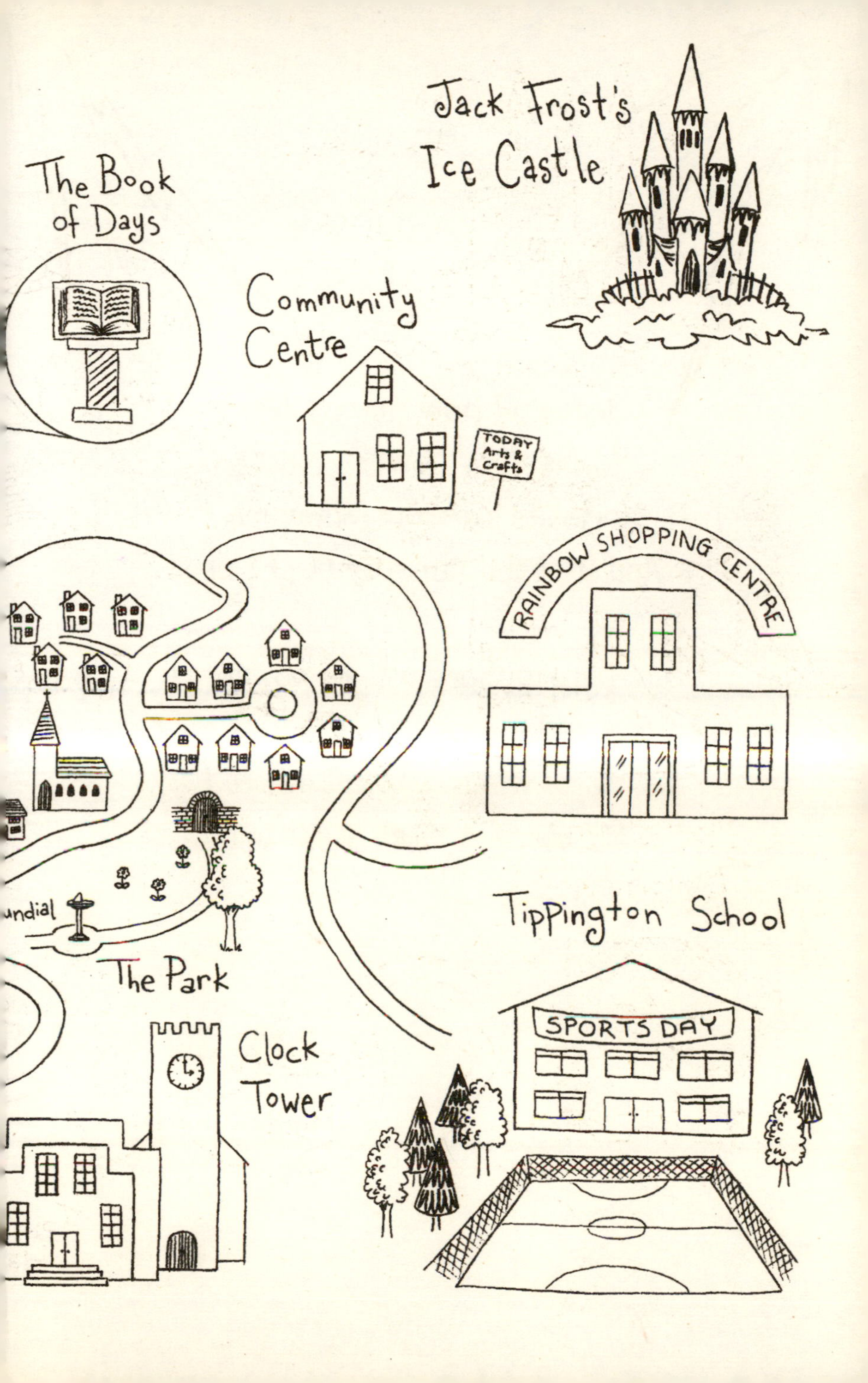

Jack Frost's Ice Castle
The Book of Days
Community Centre
TODAY Arts & Crafts
RAINBOW SHOPPING CENTRE
Tippington School
undial
The Park
Clock Tower
SPORTS DAY

Icy wind now fiercely blow!
To the Time Tower I must go.
Goblin servants follow me
And steal the Fun Day Flags I need.

I know there will be no fun,
For fairies or humans once the flags are gone.
So, storm winds, take me where I say.
My plan for chaos starts today!

Contents

"I can't believe it's Sunday already!" Kirsty Tate said, glancing at her best friend Rachel Walker. They were in the Walkers' kitchen, wrapping sandwiches in plastic bags. "And Mum and Dad are coming to fetch me tonight," Kirsty added. "Hasn't this week gone quickly?"

"Yes, it has," Rachel agreed. "That's because we've been busy looking for the fairies' Fun Day Flags!"

Just then Mr Walker hurried in, carrying a large wicker picnic basket. Rachel stopped talking immediately and grinned at Kirsty. Nobody else knew that the two girls had a magical secret: they were friends with the fairies!

For the last week the two girls had been trying to find the missing Fun Day Flags and return them to the seven Fun Day Fairies. The flags were very important because the fairies used their magic to make every day of the week fun. Naughty Jack Frost and his goblin servants had stolen the flags, but the flags' special magic meant that the goblins had fun all the time instead of working. Jack Frost had become so annoyed that he cast a spell and banished the flags to the human world. However, his cheeky goblin servants had missed having fun so much that, unknown to Jack Frost, they had sneaked away to try and get the flags back.

"Let's pack the food, girls," said Mr Walker, putting the picnic basket on the table. "We want to get off early so that we can make the most of this sunny weather."

"It's a brilliant idea to have a picnic at Windy Lake, Dad," Rachel said, as she popped a plastic container of salad into the basket.

"And all this food looks delicious," Kirsty added, looking at a large peach pie.

"Put the pie and sandwiches in last or they'll get squashed," Mr Walker suggested as the girls added bottles of water to the basket.

"Will you finish packing while I get the car out of the garage?"

Kirsty and Rachel nodded.

"We've only got Sarah the Sunday Fairy's flag left to find now," Rachel said, when Mr Walker had gone.

"Yes, but this is the last flag. So the goblins will be even more determined to find it," Kirsty pointed out.

Rachel put a picnic blanket on top of the food and closed the basket as Mrs Walker came in.

"That looks heavy, Rachel," she said. "Leave it for your dad to carry. I'm just going to get Buttons in from the garden."

Rachel and Kirsty ran upstairs to get their jackets. As they came downstairs, Mr Walker staggered out of the kitchen, carrying the picnic basket with both hands.

"This basket weighs a ton!" he groaned. "Did you pack a peach pie for us each, girls?"

Kirsty and Rachel laughed as Mrs Walker and Buttons joined them. The shaggy dog sniffed the air and then launched himself at the picnic basket, barking excitedly.

"Calm down, Buttons!" Rachel said, pulling him back. "I put some biscuits in for you, but you must wait until we get to Windy Lake."

They all climbed into the car and set off. Buttons yelped eagerly at the picnic basket throughout the journey.

"It's lucky it's not far to Windy Lake," Rachel laughed. After a short drive, Mr Walker turned off the main road onto a narrow, bumpy track.

As they reached the end of the track, Kirsty gasped with delight. "Oh, this is great!" she cried.

In front of them was a large, shimmering, horseshoe-shaped lake, surrounded by lush green woods. A few other people were picnicking, walking their dogs and feeding the ducks on the lake, but the girls could see that they weren't having much fun.

"We need to find the Sunday flag," Rachel whispered, "so that the fairies can put the fun back into Sunday."

Kirsty nodded as Mr Walker parked the car and they all climbed out.

"That's a good spot for a picnic," said Rachel's mum, pointing to a shady tree near the water's edge. They went over to it, with Buttons still pulling frantically at his lead and Mr Walker carrying the picnic basket.

"I think Buttons needs a walk to calm him down," Mr Walker panted, putting the basket down with a sigh of relief. "Why don't you girls unpack the picnic while we take him for a quick run?"

"Good idea," said Mrs Walker, taking the lead from Rachel.

Buttons trotted reluctantly after Mr and Mrs Walker, glancing back at the picnic basket every so often.

"I wonder what's wrong with Buttons," Rachel said. "I've never seen him like that before—" Suddenly, she stopped and frowned. "What's that rustling noise?"

Kirsty pointed at the picnic basket. "I think it's coming from in there," she whispered.

"It might be Sarah the Sunday Fairy!" Rachel said, excitedly, carefully lifting the lid of the basket.

She and Kirsty peeped inside and then both girls cried out in surprise. There sat a big green goblin holding a sandwich in his hands, which he was clearly just about to gobble up!

A Second Stowaway

"That's my ham salad sandwich!" Rachel gasped, grabbing the sandwich out of the goblin's hand just as he was taking a bite.

All he got was a mouthful of air, and he glared furiously at Rachel. "Give that back!" he demanded gruffly.

"No, it's not yours!" Rachel replied, hiding the sandwich behind her back.

"What are you doing in our picnic basket, anyway?" added Kirsty.

"I'm not going to tell you!" the goblin muttered sulkily.

"Why not?" asked Rachel.

"Because I'm not going to tell you anything," the goblin said firmly. "I'm especially not going to tell you that we're looking for the Sunday Fun Flag, because you're not allowed to know about that!" Then he frowned and clapped a hand over his mouth.

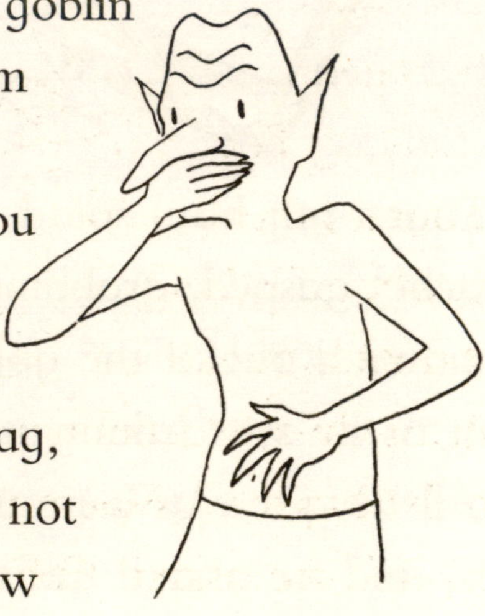

"Too late!" Rachel said cheerfully. "You've just told us."

Scowling, the goblin grabbed a chocolate biscuit, jumped out of the basket and scurried away into the trees.

"I wonder if that means the Sunday flag is around here somewhere?" Kirsty said thoughtfully.

Meanwhile, Rachel was peering into the basket. "Where is the picnic blanket?" she asked. "The goblin must have taken it out to make room for himself!"

"No wonder Buttons was so excited," Kirsty said. "He must have smelled the goblin inside the basket."

"I hope the goblin hasn't eaten a lot of food!" Rachel said, taking out the packets of sandwiches and checking them. "How will we explain that to Mum and Dad?"

The girls unpacked the basket, but none of the food seemed to be missing except the one chocolate biscuit the goblin had stolen.

"Looks like we found him just in time," Kirsty laughed. Then suddenly she clutched Rachel's arm. "Look!" she gasped. "I can see magic sparkles!"

Rachel's heart began to pound. She too could see dazzling silver sparkles drifting up from behind an apple in the corner of the basket.

Carefully Kirsty moved the apple aside. Behind it sat an untidy little fairy, her long black hair tangled and messy. She saw the girls looking down at her and waved at them with her wand.

Then she jumped to her feet, shook out her short yellow dress and smoothed her shiny hair.

"Hello, girls," she called, "It's me, Sarah the Sunday Fairy. Thanks for getting rid of the goblin; I was getting really squashed!"

"Hello, Sarah," Rachel said happily as the fairy stretched her crumpled wings and fluttered out of the basket.

"We think the goblin being here might mean your flag's nearby."

Sarah nodded eagerly. "Yes, you're right," she said. "The Book of Days has given us a clue."

In Fairyland, the Book of Days was checked every morning by Francis the Frog, the Fairyland Royal Time Guard, so that he could fly the correct day's flag at the top of the Time Tower in the palace gardens. When the sun struck the flag, the Fun Day Fairy in charge of that day of the week would recharge her wand in its magic rays. But since the flags had gone, poems had appeared in the Book of Days giving clues to the whereabouts of the flags.

Sarah recited:

"The Sunday flag likes picnic fun.
You're sure to find it in the sun.
Jack Frost's goblins want it too,
So getting it first is up to you!"

"I think the goblins must have been hiding somewhere in the courtyard when Francis read out the poem, so they overheard it," Sarah explained. "That's why one of them hid in your picnic basket."

"We'll just have to make sure we find the flag first," Kirsty said.

Sarah nodded. "We must be careful though," she added. "I'm sure there are lots more goblins around. After all, this is their last chance to get hold of a Fun Day Flag!"

"Woof!" came a happy bark from behind them.

Rachel glanced round to see her mum, dad and Buttons coming towards them. "Sarah, you'd better hide," she whispered.

Quickly Sarah zoomed over to Kirsty, and hid in her pocket.

"I think Buttons has worked off some of his excess energy," laughed Mrs Walker as they joined the girls.

"We saw a man flying a fantastic kite on the other side of the lake," Mr Walker added. "It was a big red dragon with a long blue tail. Keep an eye out for it."

Rachel's mum was looking puzzled. "Where's the blanket, Rachel?" she asked.

"Oh, er, I must've forgotten to put it in," said Rachel quickly. She couldn't tell her mum that a goblin must have thrown it out!

"Not to worry," said Mrs Walker. "There's a blanket in the car. I left it on the parcel shelf after the Craft Fair on Wednesday. Will you fetch it?"

She handed Rachel the keys and the girls set off for the car.

As they came within sight of it, Rachel blinked, unable to believe her eyes. It looked as though someone was standing on the roof.

Suddenly, Rachel realised what it was. "There's a goblin on the roof!" she exclaimed in surprise.

"And there are two of them standing on the boot," Kirsty added.

"And another two on the bonnet as well!" whispered Sarah.

The goblins were peering intently into the Walkers' car. As Sarah and the girls got closer, they saw that there were two more goblins, one standing on the other's shoulders so that he could look in through a side window.

"That makes seven goblins altogether," Rachel said, sounding anxious.

"What are they looking at?" Kirsty asked.

The girls crept up quietly behind the goblins to find out.

"Let me have a look!" the goblin who was holding the other one up was complaining. "My turn now!"

Very carefully, so as not to alert the goblins, Rachel peeped into the car herself. She could see the striped blanket her mother had mentioned lying on the parcel shelf, but poking out from underneath it was some silver fabric with a glittering sun pattern on it.

"Oh!" Rachel whispered. "I think the Sunday flag is inside our car!"

Sarah and Kirsty looked where Rachel was pointing. Then they all hurried to hide behind a big oak tree before the goblins noticed them.

"It is my flag!" Sarah said excitedly.

"But the goblins have found it now," Kirsty said. "What are we going to do?"

"Well, the flag's safe inside the car," Rachel said. "But how are we going to get it out?"

"We'll have to get the goblins away from the car." Kirsty said thoughtfully. "But how?"

"Look!" one of the goblins shouted just then.

The girls peered round the tree to see what was happening. The goblin standing on the car roof was pointing up at the sky looking excited.

"What's he pointing at?" asked Kirsty.

She and Rachel stared across the lake. There in the distance they could see a red and blue kite, shaped like a dragon, swooping and soaring on the breeze.

"It's the kite Dad was talking about," Rachel whispered.

"I can see a kite shaped like a dragon!" the goblin shouted gleefully. "But you lot can't! Ha ha ha!"

The other goblins scowled. "I want to see it!" one moaned.

"Let me have a look!" cried another.

Pushing and shoving, the other six goblins climbed up onto the roof of the car to see the kite for themselves.

"We could try to get the flag while they're watching the kite..." Rachel suggested.

But then the goblins gave a loud groan.

"The pretty kite's gone behind that big tree," one of them grumbled, sliding off the roof.

"We mustn't waste any more time," another goblin pointed out. "How are we going to get the flag out of this car?"

"That kite's given me an idea!" Kirsty whispered, her face glowing with excitement. "Sarah, could you magic a wonderful kite? I bet that would distract the goblins."

Sarah grinned. "What a brilliant idea!" she said, and fluttered up into the air to wave her wand.

There was a burst of magic sparkles above the girls' heads, and a golden string appeared in Kirsty's hand. The girls looked up and high in the sky, at the end of the string, was a beautiful golden kite shaped like a phoenix. It had a long rainbow-coloured tail that swished back and forth as the kite looped this way and that.

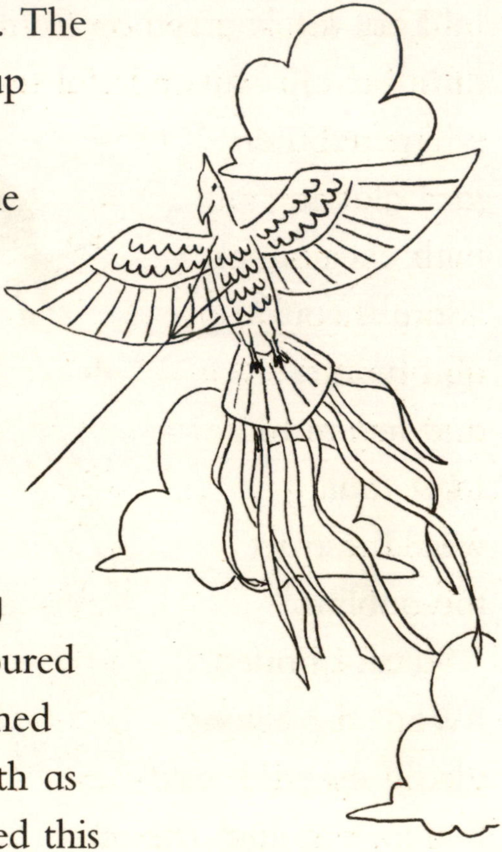

Kirsty stepped out from behind the car so that the goblins could see the kite. "This kite is great fun!" she said loudly, making the kite swoop from side to side. "I'm having a wonderful time!"

The goblins stared at the kite, their eyes wide. Soon, they forgot all about the flag and began to move away from the car towards Kirsty.

"Can I have a go?" the biggest goblin asked.

"No, me first!" another shouted, pushing him out of the way.

"You can all have a turn," said Kirsty, handing the string to the nearest goblin.

Meanwhile Sarah and Rachel sneaked over to the Walkers' car. Her heart thumping, Rachel quietly unlocked the door, reached in and grabbed the flag. She tried to shut the door quietly, but one of the goblins heard the noise and looked round.

"Hey!" he shrieked. "They're taking the flag!"

The goblin holding the kite string let go, and all seven goblins charged back to the car. Anxiously, Kirsty followed them as they surrounded Sarah and Rachel.

"Give that to me!" One of the goblins snapped. He tried to grab the flag, but Rachel held it up out of his reach.

"Rachel, look out!" Kirsty cried, as she saw another of the goblins scrambling up onto the roof of the car.

But she was too late. The goblin reached down and whipped the flag straight out of Rachel's hand!

A Frosty Fake

"I've got the flag!" the goblin cackled with glee. Then he jumped down from the car and ran off into the woods, followed by the others.

"After them!" Rachel gasped.

The girls followed the goblins into the woods with Sarah zooming alongside. But the goblins were fast runners, and

Rachel and Kirsty were soon out of breath, especially as the goblins kept dodging in and out of the trees.

"We have to make them stop," Kirsty panted. "But how?"

"I know what would slow them down," Rachel said breathlessly. "Jack Frost!"

Kirsty and Sarah looked puzzled.

"The goblins aren't supposed to be looking for the flags, are they?" Rachel pointed out. "So they'll be terrified if an angry Jack Frost appears – or if they see something which they think is Jack Frost!"

Sarah grinned. "I can't make a Jack Frost lookalike appear out of thin air," she said, "but I can make something else look like Jack Frost."

Sarah pointed her wand at an old tree stump a little way ahead of the goblins. A stream of silver sparkles shot from the wand and surrounded the stump.

Immediately it seemed to change shape, becoming a spiky, icy-looking figure with a stern frown.

The goblin at the front of the crowd suddenly skidded to a halt. "It's Jack Frost!" he gasped.

All the other goblins bumped heavily into the back of him, then huddled together looking terrified.

"Hello, master," one goblin muttered nervously. "How, er, nice to see you."

"It wasn't my fault," another whined. "It was their idea to look for the flag."

The goblin holding the flag looked the most scared of all. He hurried forward and bowed to the tree stump. "The flag is a special present for you, master," he said, holding it out.

Then he frowned and peered more closely at the tree stump. He poked it hard, and all the goblins gasped.

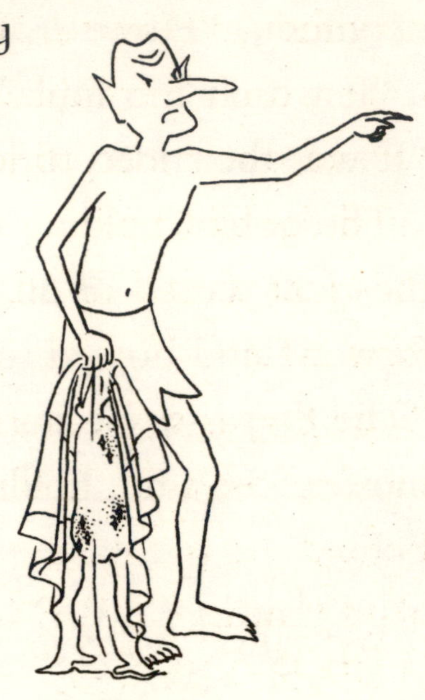

"It's not Jack Frost!" the goblin shouted, looking very relieved. "It's just an old tree stump!"

The goblins looked puzzled, but then one of them spotted Sarah and the girls just behind them.

"Fairy magic!" he shouted, pointing at them.

"Ha!" jeered the goblin with the flag. "You don't fool us!"

Sarah, Rachel and Kirsty glanced at each other in dismay. But at that moment a chill wind swirled out of nowhere and an icy figure appeared behind the goblins.

"It's Jack Frost!" Kirsty cried. "He's behind you."

"I told you, we're not fooled that easily," scoffed the goblin with the flag.

Behind the gloating goblins, Jack Frost looked furious. "GIVE ME THAT FLAG!" he bellowed.

The Real Jack Frost

Unable to believe their ears, the goblins spun round to face Jack Frost.

"GIVE ME THAT FLAG!" Jack Frost roared again. And he waved his wand, sending icy lightning bolts shooting all round the clearing.

Pale with fright, the goblins scattered, diving behind rocks and tree trunks.

The one holding the flag was so scared that he dropped it on the ground in front of Jack Frost and jumped into the middle of a bush.

Sarah, Rachel and Kirsty also dashed behind a tree, dodging the flying lightning bolts.

"I've had enough of this!" Jack Frost snapped, picking up the flag. "I've been sitting in my castle, calling for my slippers, but nobody brought them! And shall I tell you why?" He shook the flag. "Because all my goblins are off, searching for this silly flag!"

Quickly he rounded up his goblins, who stood very sheepishly in front of him.

"Please, sir," the biggest goblin said. "Now that we've got the flag, we can all go back to the ice castle, and we'll bring you your slippers whenever you want!"

Sarah looked dismayed. "We can't let Jack Frost take the flag back to his ice castle, girls," she said anxiously. "We must stop him."

Rachel and Kirsty exchanged a determined look and then stepped bravely from behind the tree. Their knees shook as Jack Frost glared at them.

"If you take the flag back to your castle, the goblins will have so much fun they'll start playing pranks again," Rachel told Jack Frost.

"Have you forgotten about that trick they played on you when the bucket of water fell on your head?"

Jack Frost frowned.

"And when you call for your slippers, the goblins will probably fill them with mud for a joke!" Kirsty added. "Are you sure you want the flag?"

Jack Frost looked furious but thoughtful. He was clearly thinking about what the girls had said.

Rachel and Kirsty waited, trying not to shiver in the freezing air. What would Jack Frost decide?

A Perfect Picnic

Suddenly Jack Frost stepped forward. "Take the flag!" he snapped, handing it to Rachel. "But the fairies must promise to keep the Fun Day Flags safe, and never ever let the goblins touch them again!" He glared at Sarah. "Do you promise?" he demanded.

Sarah grinned. "I promise," she replied firmly.

Jack Frost nodded and turned to his troop of goblins. "Quick march!" he shouted.

Sarah, Kirsty and Rachel couldn't help smiling as the goblins trudged after Jack Frost, looking extremely glum.

"Thank you, girls," Sarah laughed. "Now I have my precious flag back!" She waved her wand over it and the flag immediately shrank down to its Fairyland size.

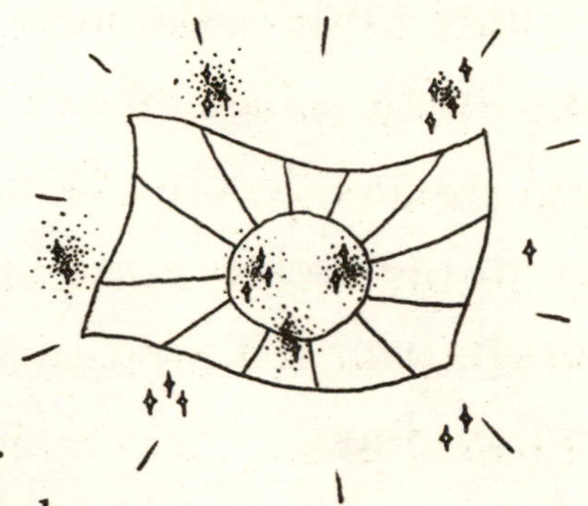

"What happened to the magic kite?" asked Kirsty, staring up into the air.

"It dissolved magically in the breeze," Sarah explained with a smile. "And now, why don't you come back to Fairyland with me to give everyone the good news?"

"We'd love to," Rachel replied. "But my parents will soon start wondering where we are."

"Don't worry, I'll send you back so that hardly any time has passed in the human world," the little fairy promised. And, with a flick of her wand, Kirsty and Rachel became fairies again, and found themselves zooming along with Sarah, over the pretty toadstool houses of Fairyland.

Looking down, the girls could see lots of fairies in the palace gardens.

"What's happening?" Rachel asked curiously.

"They're having a picnic!" Sarah laughed.

As they flew closer to the ground, Kirsty and Rachel could see that the fairies, including King Oberon and Queen Titania, were sitting in the Time Tower courtyard on soft blankets spun from silvery cobweb threads.

They were surrounded by golden plates piled with sandwiches, cakes and biscuits. But the girls could see that nobody was having much fun.

"Look!" cried Francis the Frog, hurrying forward with the Book of Days in his arms. "It's Sarah, Rachel and Kirsty, and they have the Sunday Fun Flag!"

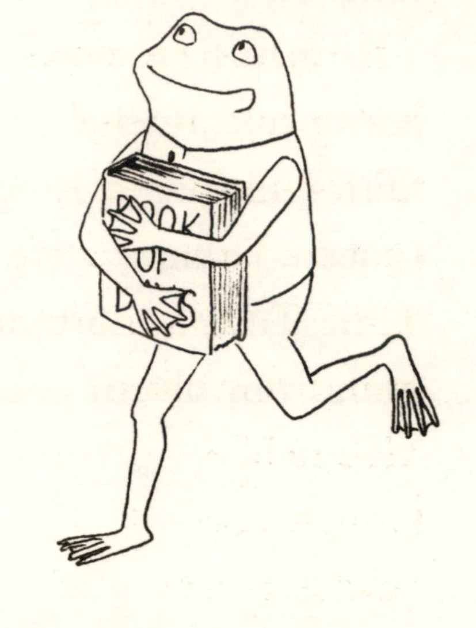

The fairies clapped joyfully as Sarah and the girls fluttered to the ground.

"Welcome, Rachel and Kirsty," Queen Titania said sweetly. "Once again we cannot thank you enough for all your help!"

"And now Sarah must recharge her wand with Fun Day Magic," King Oberon added, "or Sunday will be over and we won't have had any fun at all!"

Everyone watched as Sarah ran over to stand at the centre of the giant clock in the middle of the courtyard. Meanwhile, Francis hopped quickly inside the Time Tower. A moment later everyone cheered as he hauled the Sunday flag to the top of the flagpole.

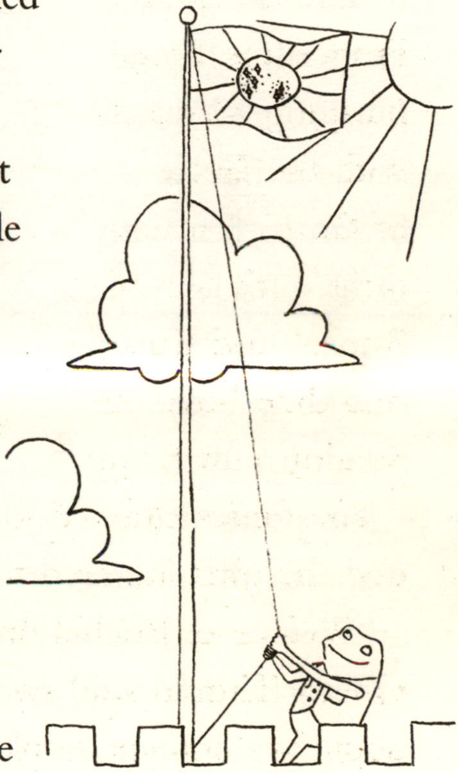

"Here comes the Fun Day Magic!" Kirsty said to Rachel, as the sun's rays struck the flag.

Sarah held up her wand and as the magical, reflected rays poured down towards her, it began to fizz with silver sparkles. "Now Sundays can be fun again!" Sarah laughed.

She pointed her wand at the courtyard and sent a sparkling cloud of Fun Day Magic streaming over the whole picnic. Suddenly, shiny paper chains and glittery balloons

decorated the trees, and a huge plate of fairy cakes iced in pink, blue, yellow and green appeared in a flash of magic.

"We have all our Fun Day Flags again, thanks to you, girls," said Queen Titania as the seven Fun Day Fairies gathered round her.

"And the Book of Days is back to normal, too," declared Francis happily as he hurried out of the Time Tower.

"You must join our picnic," King Oberon added.

"Thank you," Rachel said gratefully. "But we have our own picnic to eat back at Windy Lake. We don't want to spoil our appetites."

King Oberon smiled. "Oh, but think how small one of our fairy cakes will be when you're human-sized again!" he pointed out.

The girls laughed and took a fairy cake each. As they ate, they watched the fairies dancing and they even got to join in playing party games. Everyone was having such fun that Kirsty and Rachel were sorry when it was time to leave.

"Sarah will go with you to the human world to put some Fun Day Magic back into Sunday," Queen Titania told them. "And look out for a special fairy surprise back at the lake!"

"Thank you once again, my dears," said King Oberon. "And goodbye."

All the fairies clustered round Kirsty and Rachel. "Goodbye and thank you!" they cried.

Then Sarah waved her wand, and she, Kirsty and Rachel left for Windy Lake in a mist of magic sparkles.

"Let's find the blanket, Rachel," said Kirsty, as they arrived back at the Walkers' car.

"And I have Fun Day Magic to work," said Sarah, spinning happily in the air. "Goodbye, girls."

Kirsty and Rachel waved as the fairy fluttered away. Then they collected the picnic blanket from the car and hurried back to the lake.

As the girls neared their picnic spot, Buttons rushed to meet them along with Rachel's dad.

"Girls," Mr Walker called breathlessly, "look what just landed near us!" He held out two beautiful kites. One was pink, the other yellow, and they glittered in the sun, just like the Fun Day Flags. Both the kites had long, rainbow-coloured tails.

"Read the messages on them," Mr Walker went on.

The girls saw that both kites had messages tied to their tails which read:

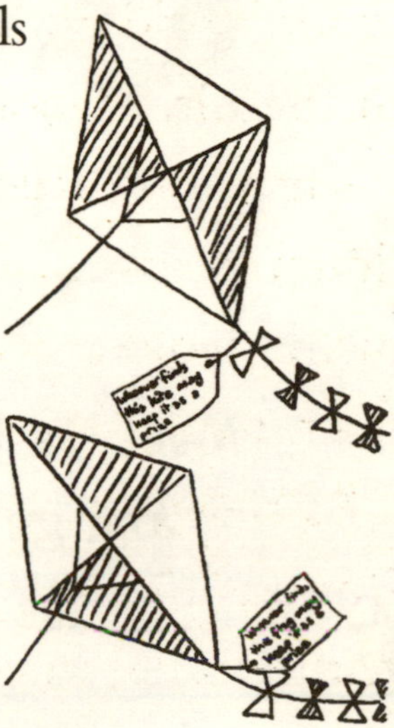

Whoever finds this kite
may keep it as a prize.
We hope it brings
delight, swooping
through the skies!

"Isn't that lucky?" Rachel's dad beamed at them. "You can have a kite each! Shall we try them out now?"

Rachel and Kirsty grinned at each other in delight, knowing that this must be the surprise that the Fairy Queen had promised them. They both felt very lucky to have such wonderful fairy friends.

Meet the fairies, play games
and get sneak peeks at
the latest books!

There's fairy fun for everyone at

www.rainbowmagicbooks.co.uk

You'll find great activities, competitions, stories and fairy profiles, and also a special newsletter.